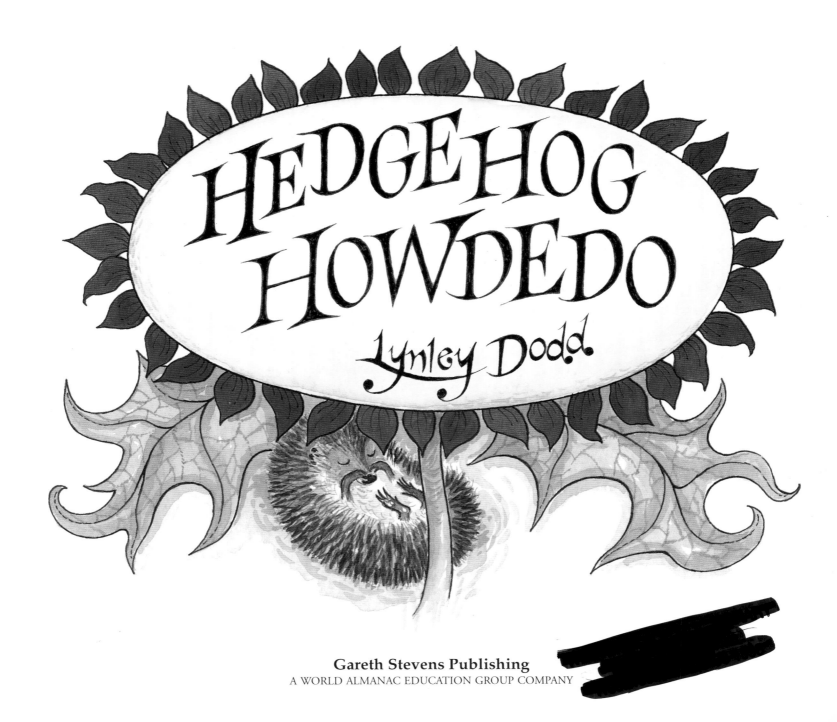

HEDGEHOG HOWDEDO

Lynley Dodd

Gareth Stevens Publishing
A WORLD ALMANAC EDUCATION GROUP COMPANY

My garden's FULL of hedgehogs.
They're sleeping two by three,
under every flower,

every bush,

There's one beneath the Pizza plant.

five beside the shed,

and six are sweetly snoozing
in the Cockleberry bed.

and eight are snoring loudly
in the woodpile,
bold as brass.

I can't think WHAT will happen,
in just a month or two,
to the horde of hibernators
in this hedgehog howdedo.

in spring.

Please visit our web site at: **www.garethstevens.com**
For a free color catalog describing Gareth Stevens' list of high-quality books and multimedia programs, call 1-800-542-2595 (USA) or 1-800-461-9120 (Canada). Gareth Stevens Publishing's Fax: (414) 332-3567.

Other GOLD STAR FIRST READER Millennium Editions:

Library of Congress Cataloging-in-Publication Data

Dodd, Lynley.
    Hedgehog howdedo / by Lynley Dodd.
      p. cm. — (Gold star first readers)
      Summary: Hibernating hedgehogs introduce the numbers from one to eight in a winter garden with pizza plants and a cockleberry bed.
      ISBN 0-8368-2895-X (lib. bdg.)
      [1. Hedgehogs—Fiction. 2. Gardens—Fiction. 3. Counting. 4. Stories in rhyme.] I. Title. II. Series.
PZ8.3.D637He   2001
[E]—dc21
                                    2001020159

This edition first published in 2001 by
Gareth Stevens Publishing
A World Almanac Education Group Company
330 West Olive Street, Suite 100
Milwaukee, WI 53212 USA

First published in 2000 in New Zealand by Mallinson Rendel Publishers Ltd. Original © 2000 by Lynley Dodd.

Printed in the United States of America

1 2 3 4 5 6 7 8 9 05 04 03 02 01